RECON ACADEMY

FILE NO. 87DH58

NUCLEAR DISTRACTION

BY CHRIS EVERHEART
ILLUSTRATED BY ARCANA STUDIO

ACCESS GRANTED »»

STONE ARCH BOOKS
MINNEAPOLIS SAN DIEGO

Recon Academy is published by Stone Arch Books
151 Good Counsel Drive, P.O. Box 669
Mankato, Minnesota 56002
www.stonearchbooks.com

Library of Congress Cataloging-in-Publication Data
Everheart, Chris.
Nuclear Distraction / by Chris Everheart; illustrated by Arcana Studio.
p. cm. — (Recon Academy)
ISBN 978-1-4342-1167-5 (library binding)
ISBN 978-1-4342-1381-5 (pbk.)
1. Graphic novels. [1. Graphic novels. 2. Terrorism—Fiction.] I. Arcana Studio. II. Title.
PZ7.7.E94Nuc 2009
[Fic]—dc22 2008032457

Summary: At a karate tournament, Hazmat loses his match but scores his first date. But as a member of the Recon Academy, this forensics expert has more to worry about than what to wear. The evil Shadow Cell squadron has broken into the city's nuclear power plant. If the Recon Academy doesn't hurry, a massive meltdown might ruin Hazmat's big night.

Designer: Bob Lentz
Series Editor: Donnie Lemke
Series Concept: Michael Dahl, Brann Garvey, Heather Kindseth, Donnie Lemke

1 2 3 4 5 6 14 13 12 11 10 09

Printed in the United States of America

TABLE OF CONTENTS

ENTER

Born into a world of rising threat —

— they witnessed terror strike the safety of their town.
FEDERAL B

As they grew up, each member developed a unique ability . . .

FORENSICS

MARTIAL ARTS

COMPUTERS
GADGETRY

In the halls of Seaside High, the four of them united.
SEASIDE HIGH SCHOOL
They combined their skills and formed the most high-tech and secret security force on Earth.
RECON ACADEMY
CONTINUE

SECTION

FILE NO.
87DHS8

ACCESS GRANTED

HAZMAT
FORENSICS

128718
293829
9283
98289
89
1
109201
192091
1992

Early one Saturday afternoon, in downtown Seaside . . .
SEASIDE
CIVIC CENTER
KARATE TOURNAMENT
Fight!
Come on, Hazmat!
Zuki!
Zuki?
Huh?
Point!
WHAP!
Oof!

Zuki means punch, remember?
And keep your eyes on your opponent!

Now, gari!
Gari!

What does that mean?

Kick!

HI-YAH!
THWAP!!
Point!
All right, Hazmat!

That kick was perfect!
Now, *ashi barai!*

Speak English, Emmi!

Do the foot sweep! Quick, before — !

THUD

Ouch!
Winner! Alex White!
Ugh.

What happened?
Ashi barai.

He got you with a foot sweep.
I can't believe I let you talk me into joining this tournament.

Martial arts are perfect for working on your hand-to-hand combat skills.

RING!
RING!
RING!
It doesn't feel perfect. It hurts!

I'm getting a text message from Ryker.
He just issued a security alert.
Uh-oh! It's a Code-4.
I better find a secure frequency and call him back.
ENT

SECTION

FILE NO.
87DHS8

ACCESS GRANTED

HAZMAT
FORENSICS

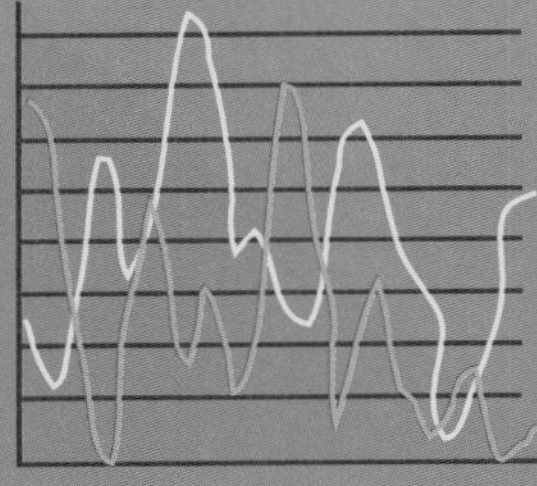

Moments later . . .
BUZZ
BUZZ
BUZZ
Emmi, where are you guys?
I've been trying to contact you for an hour.
We're at the karate tournament in downtown Seaside.
The reception is terrible.
We're in the basement of the Civic Center.
Hold on. I'll boost the signal.
CLICK
CLICK
CLICK
Is that better?

I hear you loud and clear.
Now what's going on?
There's a security breach at the nuclear power plant.

Hey, guys. This is Jay.
I'm uploading our digital surveillance.

As you'll see, the breach is in the southeast corner of the building.
Looks like an air vent was opened.

Got it, Jay.
I'm also sending a live image from the plant's security camera.

The infrared isn't detecting anyone inside the van.
The crooks are probably in the power plant already.

Shadow Cell?
Who else?

Okay, we'll meet you guys at the plant.

Matthew Hazner?

I'm Alex White, your opponent in the last match.
You're a, uh —
She's a girl, Hazmat.
That was a good match.
Thanks. You too.
Anyway, I was wondering if you're staying for the banquet after the tournament tonight.
Well, I kind of have to take off right now.
Haz, I think she's asking you on a date.

I mean, I'm busy right now.
But I could probably be back for the banquet.

Great! I'll save a seat for you.

Okay, see you at seven!
Come on, lover boy.

FILE NO. 87DHS8

SECTION

ACCESS GRANTED

HAZMAT
FORENSICS

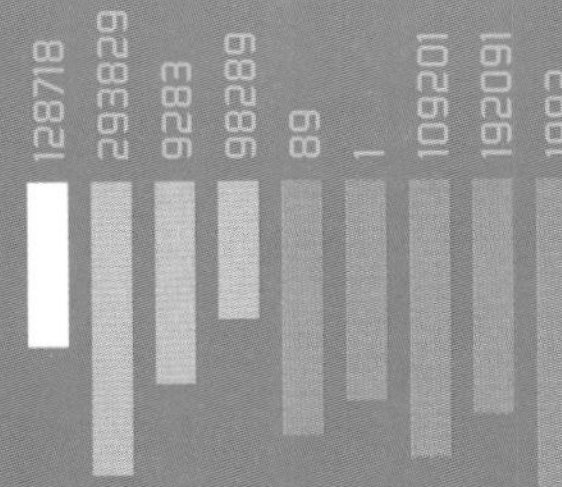

Soon . . .
Hurry up, Haz!
There's trouble at the power plant, remember?
I know, but a girl asked me out!
Yeah, after she kicked your butt.
Are you jealous or something?
Dream on.
Outside the power plant . . .
Look! We beat Jay and Ryker here.
Let's set up an observation post before they arrive.

What do you think Shadow Cell is after?
I'm not sure.
But there's a lot of dangerous materials inside that plant.

I'm marking our location for Ryker and Jay.
Hopefully, we'll get inside before Shadow Cell can do any damage.
GUARD

I just hope we're done before the banquet tonight.

A short time later . . .

I've got a lock on Hazmat and Emmi.

They're up ahead in the brush.

Ahem! Can we focus on the mission, boys?
Shadow Cell's van is over there.
I think someone is jealous.
GUARD
I'm not jealous!
Now would you please scope out that van, Jay?
Fine.
I'm still not detecting any people inside the van. No heat readings.

It's empty, guys.
5670
3300
We need to get inside the plant and locate them.
First, we need to get all of the workers out.
And I have just the thing.

Suddenly . . .
HONK! HONK!
HONK!
What's that sound?
Oh, that's the power plant's radiation alarm.
There's a radiation leak?!
Nope. Just a little computer trick.
It'll give us time to track down Shadow Cell.

Let's go! We only have a few minutes!

Uh-oh.

SECTION 4

FILE NO. 87DH58

ACCESS GRANTED))))

HAZMAT
FORENSICS

128718
293829
9283
98289
89
1
109201
192091
1992

1827178 198291821 918298

1827178 198291821 918298

Inside the power plant's control room . . .
You know what to do, Haz.
What if I forget?
You won't.
Just follow the commands I taught you.
ZZZT!

ZZZAP!
Back off, creep!

Take that!

SNAP!
BANG!
Ah! My eyes!
POP!
POP!

Emmi, what should I do?

SMACK!

Oh, right! **Hi-yah!**

Look!
They're getting away!
Let them go, Jay.
We need to secure the power plant.
That shouldn't be a problem with Hazmat on our side.
Nice moves back there, dude.

I taught him everything he knows.
Yeah, but getting the date was all me.
You won't have a date tonight, if we don't get moving.
Haz and Jay, you guys check out the main floor.
Emmi and I will hold down the control room.
You got it, Ryker.

Moments later . . .
Come on, Jay. We need to find out why Shadow Cell is here.
There's no time for your silly gadgets.
Silly gadgets, huh? This is a laser alarm.
If anyone comes through this door, we'll know about it. 
Okay, that's pretty cool. But I have something even better.

This is an energy field scanner.
It picks up trace amounts of radiation left by human footprints.
Nice work, Haz. I'll call this into Ryker.
Ryker, this is Jay. We're tracking Shadow Cell. Over.

Jay, make sure all the exits are locked down.

Haz, find out where Shadow Cell is headed.

Good luck, buddy.

You too, Jay.

Soon . . .
Exit number four is secure, Emmi. Over.
That's all of them, Jay.
Now keep an eye out for any missing equipment or explosives.
Meanwhile . . .
Ryker, looks like Shadow Cell split up. I'm headed toward the south end of the plant. Over.
You're breaking up, Haz. Please repeat.
EXIT

Just then . . .

DANGER
HEAVY WATER
PROCESSING

Jackpot!

What did he say?
Haz, please repeat. Hazmat? Hazmat?!
DANGER
HEAVY WATER PROCESSING
FILL DRAIN

SECTION

FILE NO. 87DH58

ACCESS GRANTED

HAZMAT
FORENSICS

128718
293829
9283
98289
89
1
109201
192091
1992

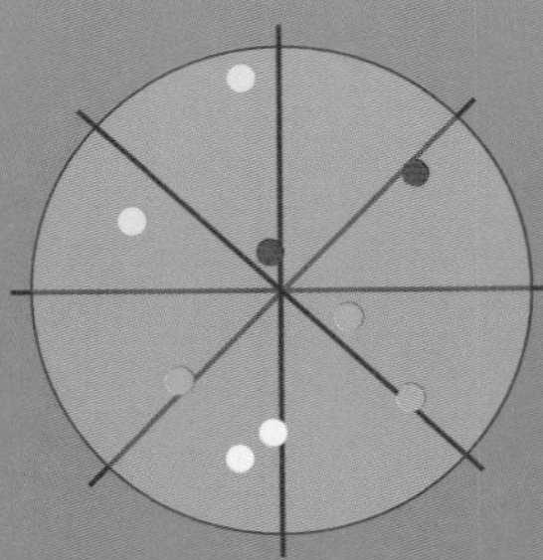

In the control room . . .
Where is he?
I don't know. I can't read his signal.
I'll try to reach Jay.
Jay, this is Emmi. Do you copy?
Loud and clear, Em.
Do you know where Haz is?
He's dropped off our radar screen.
He was following Shadow Cell's trail toward the south end of the building.

Meanwhile . . .

Control, I've got one set of footprints heading into the tank room.

Should I proceed? Over.

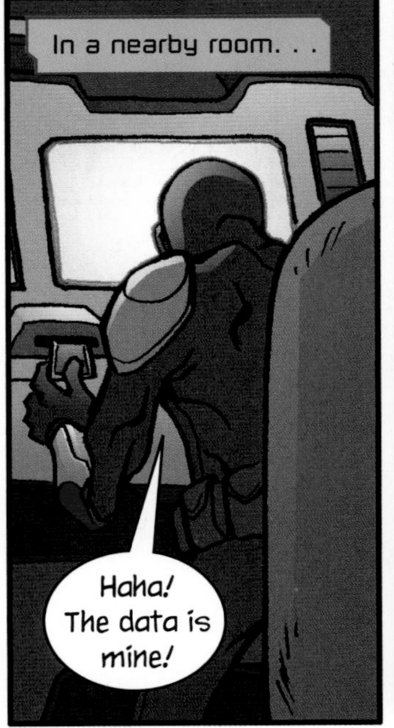

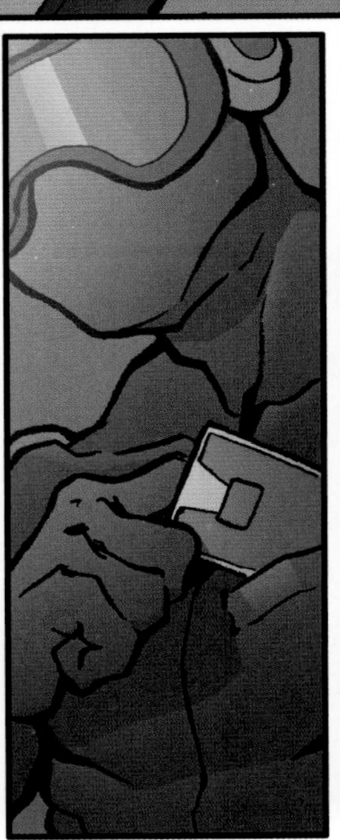

We have a security breach in the tank room.
Someone just downloaded top-secret data.

The tank room? Isn't that on the south end of the building?

Control? I need backup!

Over.
You got that right, kid.

Jay, there's one more Shadow Cell operator in the building!
We think he's in the tank room with Haz!
EXIT
Jay, get over there!
I'm on my way!

Bring it on!

What was downloaded?

Plans for the nuclear reactor. They could destroy the city with those files.

Meanwhile . . .

HIIYAH!!

In the control room . . .
Haz, if you can hear me, that suspect has stolen top-secret files.
Recover the data, at all costs!

Ha! Missed me.
Ryker, I've got the video feed from the tank room.

HIIYAH!!

Hey! I taught him that move.
Come on, Em. We need to get that data back.

Yeah, and help our friend.

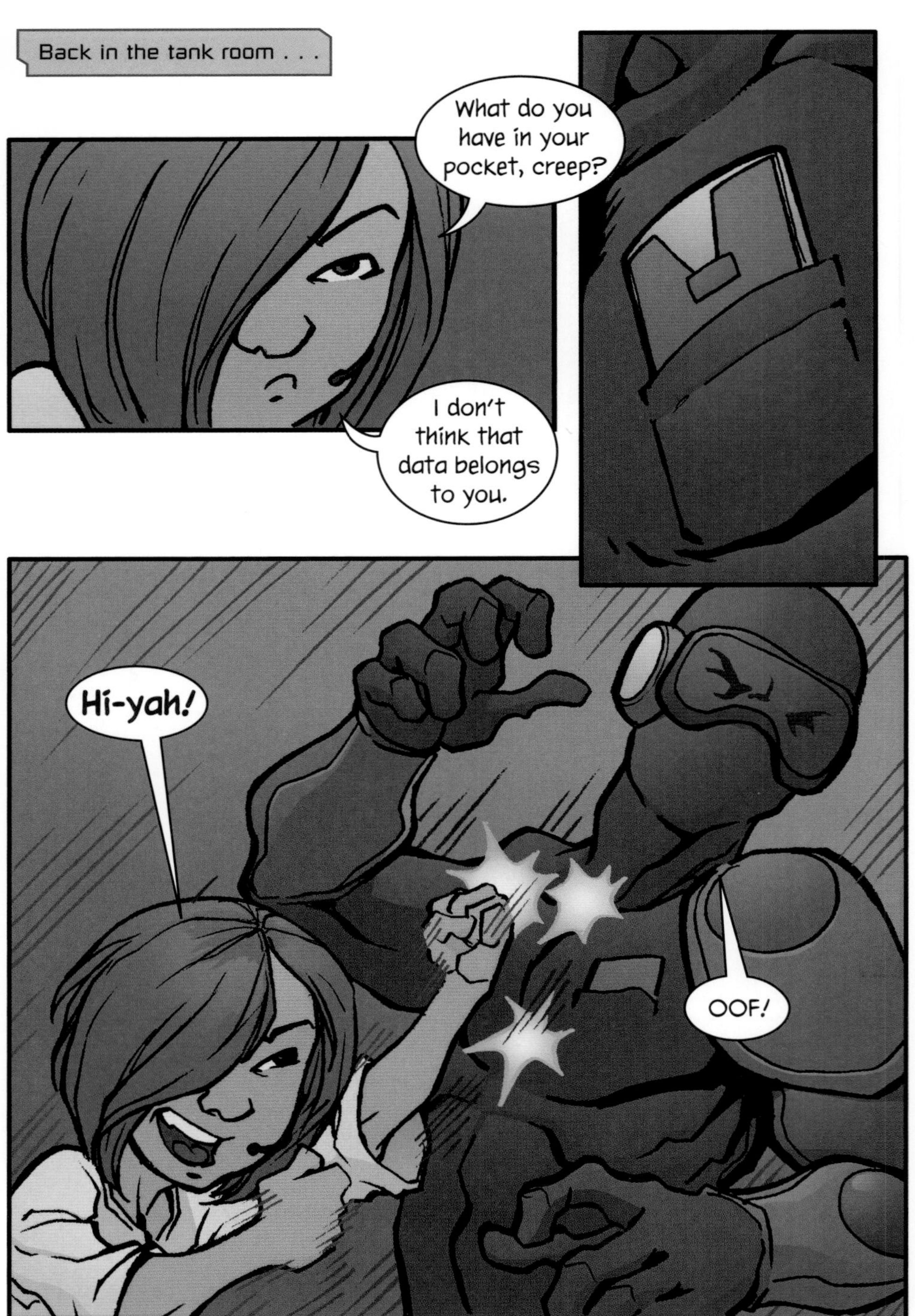
Back in the tank room . . .
What do you have in your pocket, creep?
I don't think that data belongs to you.
Hi-yah!
OOF!

RRRRRIP
So long, punk!
WHOOSH!
SPLASH!
Hahaha!

FILE NO. 87DHS8

SECTION

ACCESS GRANTED

HAZMAT
FORENSICS

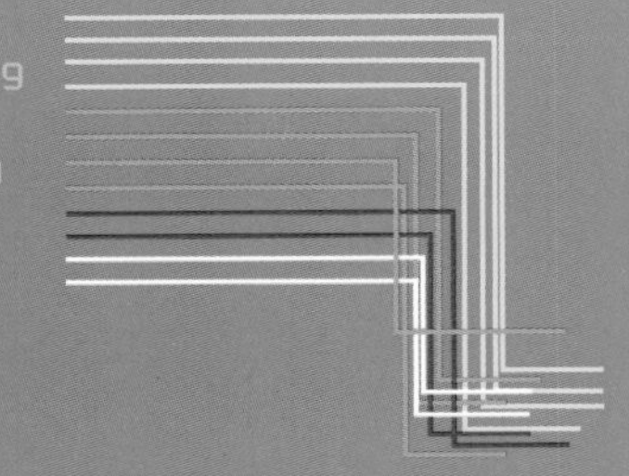

A moment later . . .
Jay, we're almost to the tank room. Where are you?
I just arrived.
But there's no one here!
Impossible! There was a download here a minute ago.
And where's Haz?
TANK
FILL DRAIN

GURGLE
GURGLE
GURGLE

Look! He's down there!

Ryker, drain the tank!

Jay, we have to get him out of there!

I'm coming, Haz!

Okay, the tank is draining.
Go, Jay!

KKRRRRRR

Soon . . .
I got you, buddy.
COUGH COUGH

Haz! Are you all right?

I'm better than all right. I won!

You got the data card back!

Hey, Ryker, is this water poisonous?

Only in large amounts, Jay. But you guys better shower off.
Fine with me.

I have to clean up for my hot date anyway!
Oh, brother.

SPYSPACE

a place for international spies

PROFILE

NAME: Matthew Hazner

CODE NAME: Hazmat

AGE: 13

HEIGHT: 5' 6"

WEIGHT: 125 lbs.

EYES: Brown

HAIR: Black

SPY ORG: Recon Academy

SPECIAL ABILITIES: Forensics, specializing in fingerprint analysis, ballistics, bloodstain pattern analysis, toxicology

FAVORITES: My well-organized briefcase filled with CSI-type gear (scopes, beakers, etc.)

QUOTE: "Once you eliminate the impossible, whatever remains, no matter how improbable, must be the truth." – Sir Arthur Conan Doyle

PHOTOS

HOME **SEARCH** **BROWSE** **LOGOUT**

FRIENDS

Ryker

Emmi

Jay

007

Alex

BLOG

recent posts see all

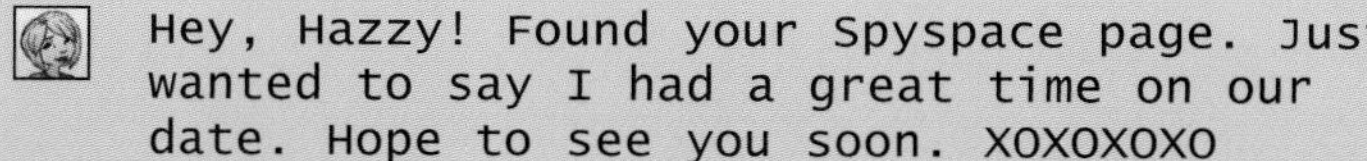

Hey, Hazzy! Found your Spyspace page. Just wanted to say I had a great time on our date. Hope to see you soon. XOXOXOXO

Ooh. I think someone's got a girlfriend...

She's not my girlfriend!

Well, it sounds like she thinks you're her boyfriend.

Really? I mean, whatever. We're just good friends.

Sure. Then why don't you let any of us call you Hazzy?

Hazmat and Alex sitting in a tree... :)

I think it's great, Haz. But how did she get onto Spyspace without an access code? This site is only for international spies.

Alex? I think we need to talk...

› EMERGENCY BRIEF

CASE: "Nuclear Distraction"
CASE NUMBER: 9781434211675
AGENT: Hazmat
ORGANIZATION: Recon Academy

SUSPECT: Nuclear technology and terrorism

OVERVIEW: A division of Shadow Cell regularly attempts to take control of nuclear technology for their criminal gains. The group is highly organized and skilled. Expect secure locales, such as the Seaside nuclear plant, to be targeted.

METHODS:
Dirty bombs (suitcase nukes)
Hijackings
Bioterrorism
Blackmail
Radiation

INTELLIGENCE:

nuclear (NOO-klee-ur)—energy or power created by splitting atoms

radioactivity (ray-dee-oh-ak-TIV-i-tee)—presence of radioactive materials emitting harmful energy

radiation poisoning (ray-dee-EY-shuhn POI-zuhn-ing)—a form of damage to skin and organ tissue caused by exposure to radiation, or nuclear waste

BACKGROUND INFORMATION:

Nuclear technology is used to create energy for a variety of purposes. The process of creating nuclear energy emits radioactive waste, which is a dangerous substance that is difficult to dispose of safely.

Radioactivity was discovered in 1898 by Marie Curie. Curie's research helped explain how radiation works, and proved that radiation exposure can be extremely dangerous depending on the dose.

Radiation poisoning is a life-threatening sickness caused by overexposure to radioactive materials, like polonium. However, smaller doses of radiation have been used effectively to destroy cancerous cells.

Dirty bombs, or suitcase nukes, are explosive devices packaged with nuclear waste. When detonated, they emit fallout, or radiation. Detonation of a dirty bomb would be disastrous.

CONCLUSION:

Nuclear technology is the most powerful source of energy on Earth — and the most deadly. Recon Academy uses education and training to prevent nuclear technology from falling into the wrong hands.

ABOUT THE AUTHOR

Chris Everheart always dreamed of interesting places, fascinating people, and exciting adventures. He is still a dreamer. He enjoys writing thrilling stories about young heroes who live in a world that doesn't always understand them. Chris lives in Minneapolis, Minnesota, with his family. He plans to travel to every continent on the globe, see interesting places, meet fascinating people, and have exciting adventures.

ABOUT THE ILLUSTRATOR

Arcana Studios, Inc. was founded by Sean O'Reilly in Coquitlam, British Columbia, in 2004. Four years later, Arcana has established itself as Canada's largest comic book and graphic novel publisher with over 100 comics and 9 books released. A nomination for a Harvey Award and winning the "Schuster Award for Top Publisher" are just a few of Arcana's accolades. The studio is known as a quality publisher for independent comic books and graphic novels.

GLOSSARY

breach (BREECH)—to break through or make a hole in something

infrared (inf-fruh-RED)—a wavelength of light that humans cannot see

opponent (uh-POH-nuhnt)—someone who is against you in a match or tournament

radiation (ray-dee-AY-shuhn)—the energy sent out from rays, heat, or light

reception (ri-SEP-shuhn)—the clarity of an electronic signal or communication

secure (si-KYOOR)—safe, or well-protected

surveillance (sur-VEY-luhns)—observation, or watching someone or something closely

DISCUSSION QUESTIONS

1. Ryker creates a false alarm in order to evacuate the power plant. Do you think this was the right thing to do? How else could he have found out what Shadow Cell was up to?

2. The Recon team members use quick thinking and athletic skills to defeat Shadow Cell. If you could be super-smart, super-strong, or a combination of both, which would you choose? Why?

3. The Recon team uses communication and teamwork to achieve their goals. What are some of the ways they use teamwork in the story to get the job done?

WRITING PROMPTS

1. Hazmat is a little nervous about using his newfound skills in karate. Have you ever been nervous about doing something new? How did you get over your nervousness? Write about your experience.

2. Imagine that you're the newest member of the Recon team. What special skills would you bring to the squad? How would you use them to help the team?

3. Each member of Recon Academy has a special skill. These skills are listed on page 4. As you read through this graphic novel, make a list of examples where each team member uses his or her skills in the field.

CHECK OUT MORE

ACTION AND ADVENTURE!

> THE HIDDEN FACE OF FREN-Z

> SHADOW CELL SCAM

> PREP SQUADRON